THE RETURN OF THE EAGLE

PAUL BUCHANAN

SADDLEBACK
PUBLISHING • INC.

TAKE TEN NOVEL SERIES

Disaster

E
Buc
C3

Sports

Mystery

Adventure

Project Editor: Liz Parker
Cover Designer and Illustrator: Marjorie Taylor
Text Illustrator: Fujiko Miller

© 1992 Saddleback Publishing, Inc.

SADDLEBACK
PUBLISHING • INC.

3505 Cadillac Ave., Building F-9
Costa Mesa, CA 92626

ISBN 1-56254-052-1
Printed in U.S.A.
  4 5 6 7 8 M 99 98 97

Chapter 1

All Jack Ford knew was that he was suddenly awake. It was still dark in his room, but he was alert. He rolled over and looked at the glowing blue numbers on his alarm clock. 2:23 A.M.

It was the heat, he told himself. It had been over a hundred every day for the last week, and the air had been windless and dry. It had been hard to sleep, even lying on top of the sheets with the window open and the electric fan spinning its face this way and that.

Jack sat up in bed.

He heard a faint rumble in the distance. At first he thought it was heat thunder, and then he began to wonder if it was the beginning of an earthquake. He was halfway out of bed, about to dive under his desk, when the distant whistle sounded. He realized that the growing rumble was a train.

The tracks passed through woods behind Jack's house and then crossed Maplethorpe Avenue about a hundred yards away. But the rails were rusted, and the wooden slats that held them together were warped and splintered. The signal arm that had once held up the traffic while the train crossed the avenue had been missing for years.

Jack had lived in Black Diamond all his life. In those fifteen years he had never heard or seen a single train on those tracks before. He had been told that they had once been used to haul lumber from the mill up in Gilbert Pass. But that was years and years ago.

The rumble of the train grew louder. Suddenly the wind chime on the back porch, which had been silent for days, furiously clanked out tinny notes. The curtains across Jack's window billowed out at him. The musty smell of steam filled his room, and then the rumble grew quiet in the distance and vanished.

For a minute Jack sat on the edge of his bed and listened to the wind chimes. There was silence again, and the air in his room grew still.

Jack lay back down on his bed. By two-thirty he was asleep again.

It wasn't until he was riding his bike across the railroad tracks on his way to school the next morning that Jack remembered the train passing in the night. He pulled his bike over on the gravel where the rails crossed Maplethorpe Avenue between the fire station and the park. Jack looked along the tracks as far as he could to where they curved and disappeared among the tall pines. The rust was still caked and flaky on the rails, and the weeds still stood tall between the wooden slats. Jack was slightly disappointed to realize that the passing train had been a dream.

By the time he reached school he had forgotten all about the night train.

It didn't quite reach one hundred degrees that day, but they still watched sports movies in P. E., instead of playing football. It had never been this hot in Black Diamond before, and the coaches were concerned that the students might get sick.

It was also too hot to think clearly. In most of Jack's classes his teachers just sat on their desks with the lights out and chatted with the students about anything that came up.

When he got home that day Jack was sweaty and drowsy. He fell asleep on the front porch with his history book and a glass of orange soda. He didn't wake up until his father came home from work.

Mr. Ford, Jack's father, owned and ran the Black Diamond Hardware Store. It wasn't a big store, but people came to it from all over because it was the only one.

At six-thirty the family sat down to dinner. Jack's older brother Dean was at basketball practice, so it was just the three of them at the table: Jack and his parents. Over a dinner of salad and ice cream (no one wanted to eat anything hot) Mr. Ford laughed about all the people who had come to the store that week to order air conditioners.

"I kept telling them that the air conditioners wouldn't be delivered for about eight weeks," he said. "By then it will be November and they'll be chopping wood to stay warm!"

Mrs. Ford laughed. "I was listening to the radio today," she said. "They said that Black Diamond hasn't had a heat wave like this for a hundred and twenty-eight years."

"Well," Jack laughed, "in another century or so, those air conditioners might come in handy."

Chapter 2

That night Jack tossed and turned in bed, but he finally fell asleep around midnight. He had been dreaming for hours when he suddenly woke up.

Although Jack knew he had been in a deep sleep, he didn't feel drowsy at all. He began to feel a faint rumble in the distance. He looked at his alarm clock. 2:25 A.M. Jack got out of bed and went to his window. He bent down and put his face close to the screen.

Out on the horizon he could see the black shadows of the tall pines against the silver of the moonlit sky. The rumble grew louder. He could feel the floorboards trembling beneath his feet. He heard the whistle blow, and then he saw the white cloud of smoke rising above the trees.

He could hear the train, but he could not see it. He heard the hissing, clanking engine. He heard the screech of the wheels on the steel tracks. He heard the rattling of the cars and the rustle of swaying trees.

Then there was silence. All that remained in the dark forest was the smoke that rose and curled among the pine branches.

Jack opened the door to his room and looked out in the hallway. There was a light on in his brother's room. He crept down and knocked on the door.

"Come in," Jack heard his brother say. Jack opened the door. Dean was propped up in his bed with pillows. He was reading a book.

"Why are you up so late?" Dean asked.

"All the noise woke me up."

"I'm not making any noise," Dean said. "So just go back to bed, you little jerk."

"Didn't you hear the racket?"

"Oh, I'm sorry if I'm turning pages too loud for you. Just stick your head under the pillow and leave me alone, will ya?"

"You mean you didn't hear the train go by?"

"Yeah, yeah," Dean said. "I heard it. It came right up the stairs and headed down the hall for your room."

"No, I'm serious. There was a train out on the tracks a minute ago. Isn't that what woke you up?"

"Nothing woke me up, Poindexter. I just can't sleep because of the heat." Dean threw one of his pillows at the doorway, but it missed Jack by a mile. "Now get your little red caboose back to dreamland before you wake up Mom and get us both in trouble."

Jack closed his brother's door and

went back to his room. He looked out his window at the pines and the stars. All he could hear was the chirping of crickets in the backyard and the occasional call of a wolf up in the hills. Jack went back to sleep.

Chapter 3

All the next day Dean made fun of Jack. By dinner everyone in the family knew about Jack's train. Jack was annoyed, but he knew that he hadn't been dreaming.

That night Jack was ready. His alarm clock woke him at two o'clock, and he jumped out of bed to turn it off before anyone heard. Jack put on his jeans, shirt, and shoes. He grabbed his flashlight.

Jack quietly opened the door to his room. He crept down the stairs, through the kitchen, and out the back door. He climbed the fence and headed into the forest.

He waited until he was well away

from the houses before he switched on the flashlight. The trees were tall and black. The beam of his tiny flashlight was only able to light up the lowest branches. He stopped when he got to the narrow clearing that had been cut more than a century ago to make way for the rails.

Jack felt in his pockets for the pennies that he had taken from his dresser. This would prove it to his brother and anyone else who doubted him. He carefully put the coins in a row along the steel rail so that the passing train would flatten them.

There wasn't much power left in his flashlight batteries, so he lit it only when he wanted to look at his watch. There was an owl in the trees across the tracks from him. Jack could see the owl twisting its head around to look at him. Crickets chirped in the forest all around. Jack looked at his watch again. It was two twenty-two.

Jack jumped when he heard a loud flapping noise. He looked up in time to see the owl rise from its branch, circle once in the moonlight, and disappear into the dark forest. The crickets fell silent. Jack looked down the tracks, and he could see a distant light threading its way among the black pines. Then the rumble began.

Jack stood and bent to look along the tracks. There was the smoke. The light grew brighter as the train raced down the tracks toward him. The ground shook and the sound thundered in his ears.

The huge black train was faster and louder than he had expected. His heart began to pound, and he ducked behind a tree. He closed his eyes and covered his ears as the great train exploded past.

Jack stayed behind the tree until he caught his breath. As he stepped back into the clearing, the crickets took up their chirping again. Jack stooped at the edge of the rail and lit his dim flashlight.

There in a row were seven untouched pennies. Jack dropped his flashlight and ran back to his house, tripping and stumbling through the black forest.

From his room he peered down upon the silent trees in the moonlight.

Chapter 4

The next day, Friday, the heat was unbearable. In Jack's fifth period algebra class Mr. Collings brought some board games from home, and everyone broke into groups to play Monopoly, Clue, and Life. Jack asked Mr. Collings if he could go to the library instead. Mr. Collings laughed. "I guess we're not studying enough for you these days," he said as he filled out a hall pass.

In the library Jack used the card catalogue to look up every book he could find about trains. He found five under *Trains*, two under *Locomotives*, and four under *Railroad*. Jack wrote down each title and number in his notebook and headed to the shelves. None of the books was there.

He rechecked each number carefully in the card catalogue and looked again on the shelves. All of them were missing. He tried the *World Book Encyclopedia*, but the volumes he wanted were gone.

Jack went over to the counter where a boy was asking the librarian a question. Jack leaned with his back to the counter waiting his turn. He looked at his watch. He had five minutes until his next class.

There was a girl with short blonde hair sitting at a table across from him. She was reading a book that was propped up against a stack of other books. She was a year older than Jack. He knew who she was, but he also knew that she didn't know him. She was popular, and Jack was not. Her name was Billie Parker. Her father was Dr. Parker, the town dentist. She was an honor student and worked on the yearbook. Jack knew that she hung out with the basketball team, because he had seen her with his brother.

Jack tilted his head to read the titles of the books in her stack. They were all about trains.

Jack went over and stood in front of her. She looked up.

"Hi," Jack said.

She smiled. "Hi."

"Are you going to be using all of those books?"

"I don't know yet. I just got them."

"Well, I kinda want to look up some stuff, and I don't have a lot of time. It's sort of imp..." Jack stopped in mid-sentence because of the odd way she was looking at him. "I was just wondering.. . ." He stopped again because the girl was staring at him with her mouth open. Jack wondered what was wrong.

"You!" the girl said excitedly. "You saw it too! Didn't you?"

"Saw what?" he asked, startled.

"The train," she said. "The night train."

Billie said she'd meet him at the flagpole after school. Jack was distracted all through his sixth period English class. They were watching *Henry V* on video tape, and he had no idea what was going on. All he could think about was talking to Billie about the train.

Mrs. Stoner let the video play a few minutes after the bell rang, so Billie was waiting at the flagpole when he got there.

"Tell me everything you saw," she said as soon as she saw him. As they walked back through school toward the bike racks, Jack told her what had happened the last few nights. She was nodding like she understood completely. When he came to the part about the pennies, she stopped walking. He turned to look at her, and she just stared at him.

"Are you sure?" she asked. "Not a single mark on them after the train went over?"

"I swear. They're probably still there if you want to see them."

They got Jack's bike from the racks and wedged it in the back seat of Billie's Nova. As they drove through town towards Jack's house, Billie told him what she had seen. She saw the train all three times from the window of her bedroom—the last time through her father's binoculars.

"I think it was a postal train."

Jack was impressed with her superior knowledge of trains—but then she *was* an honor student.

"How can you tell a postal train from another kind?" He asked shyly.

"It says U.S. MAIL on the side."

"Oh."

"The train's name was the Eagle,"

Billie went on. "At least that's what was written on the side of the engine—in old fashioned gold letters."

At the Maplethorpe crossing Billie pulled her car over on the gravel. They walked along the tracks about a quarter of a mile. Jack didn't see the pennies and was beginning to worry that he was going to make a fool of himself. Could it have been a dream after all? He was about to suggest that they turn back when Billie suddenly sprinted ahead of him. She stopped, bent over with her hands on her knees.

The pennies were there, lined up in a row along the tracks.

"This is some seriously spooky stuff," Billie said, bending to scoop up the pennies. She looked at them closely, jingled them in her hand like dice, and then handed them to Jack. He put them in his pocket. Billie bent over again to pick something up that was among the weeds at the side of the rails. She stood up waving Jack's flashlight.

"Look what I found," she said.

"Uh, that's mine," Jack said, embarrassed. "I must have left it here last night."

Billie handed him the flashlight, and they started walking back to her car.

"We need to talk to Bert Williams."

"The guy at the coffee shop? Why should we talk to him?" Jack asked.

"The guy's a train nut. He has models and pictures all over the place."

Chapter 5

Billie drove Jack back to his house. Jack asked her inside to meet his mom and to ask permission to eat dinner at the diner instead of at home. Dean was in the kitchen with Mrs. Ford.

"So," Dean said to Billie, "what's a popular girl like you doing hanging out with my stupid kid brother?"

Billie laughed. "Oh, your brother's not so bad. We're kind of working on a project together."

"Well, don't let him near any sharp instruments at the diner," Dean told her. "He's been having weird visions lately. And we're all a bit concerned."

"Dean," Mrs. Ford said sternly, "stop teasing your brother."

Bert's diner was a dark and grimy place. It wouldn't have stayed in business for a week if there was another restaurant within twenty miles. Bert was an eager and friendly man in his sixties. He was talkative, and his diner was a good place to keep up with the news.

Jack and Billie sat at the counter so that they could ask Bert questions between customers. The vinyl on Jack's stool was torn, and the stuffing was poking out. Billie ordered a cheeseburger and coffee, and Jack asked for the same, although he hated the taste of coffee.

Jack must have been in the diner a hundred times, but he had never before noticed the train lamps on the wall and the framed postcards of old steam engines. It wasn't hard for the two of them to get Bert to talk about trains; it was harder to get him to stop answering one question so they could ask him another.

"The Eagle?" Bert said, setting their cheeseburgers in front of them. "Now how did that story go?" He rubbed his chin and squinted at the ceiling. "The Eagle was a mail train, as I recall. They decided to do away with it after the Peaks Line got cut through the mountains out to the ocean."

"I don't understand," Billie said. "What difference would that make?"

"Well, the Mountain Line that ran through Black Diamond was a branch line. It only had one track that came off the Central Valley Line to cross the mountains, but the Peaks Line was a main line. She could handle a lot more traffic."

"So it was cheaper just to use the Peaks Line to the coast, huh?" Jack asked.

"Yeah," Bert said. "No sense in running two lines when you only need one."

"So where is the Eagle now? Is it still in use?" Billie asked.

Bert started laughing. "Well, believe it or not," he said, "as far as anybody knows, she's been sitting on the bottom of Morro Lake for about a hundred years now."

"The train is in Morro Lake?" Jack asked, astonished. "How did it end up in the lake?"

"Well, remember," Bert said, "they were going to close down Mountain Line. That meant they were going to lay off all the workers between the valley and Muir Point on the coast. Those were hard times. Lots of families in these parts lost their homes when the Mountain Line closed down."

Bert refilled Billie's coffee cup. He held the coffee pot over Jack's cup, ready to pour, but the cup was still full, so Bert put the coffee back on the burner. Bert continued with his story.

"Well, lots of folks were fighting mad at the Postal Service when they lost their jobs. So, the crew of the Eagle on their last trip back to the valley decided to rob her and run her off Morro Bridge."

"The Eagle was derailed by her own crew?" Jack asked.

"Yep. For years they'd find old letters and packages floating to the top of the lake any time there was a storm."

"What happened to the crew?" Jack asked.

"They got away. Left their families and headed to Canada with the loot."

"Man!" Jack said.

Bert went to wait on a customer who had just sat down at one of the tables by the front window. Jack and Billie sat in silence at the bar. Bert wandered back to the grill to fix a sandwich.

"Where did the train stop to pick up the mail at Black Diamond?" Billie asked.

"Didn't stop at all," Bert said over his shoulder from the grill. "They'd put the mail bag up on a wooden arm that hung out over the platform, and one of the Eagle's crew would just grab it as they passed by. And if there was any mail to deliver, they'd just toss it out the window of the train."

"Where was the platform?" Billie asked.

"It's still there." Bert said, turning from the grill and gesturing at the window with his knife. "It's out behind the water tower just east of town."

When they were done eating, Jack and Billie thanked Bert for his help. "Any time," Bert told them. "Any time at all. Trains are my favorite things in the world."

They were already in Billie's car with the engine running when Bert called to them from the door of the diner, wiping his hands on his apron.

"Say, if you kids are really interested in the Eagle, I can show you some articles about it. I think I've got some in my scrapbooks."

"That would be great," Billie called through the car window.

"I'll bring them in tomorrow." Bert waved as they pulled out into the street.

"What do we do now?" Jack asked.

"You think you could meet me at the water tower at about two in the morning?"

"Are you serious?" Jack asked.

"Sure am."

"I'll be there."

Chapter 6

Jack had no trouble getting out of the house, but he had made the mistake of putting his bike in the garage when he got home from school. He couldn't get it out without opening the garage door and perhaps waking someone up. He decided to walk.

When Billie had suggested going to the platform, Jack had been excited. But now, walking the quiet streets of the town in the moonlight alone, he was having second thoughts. Just the idea of seeing the ghostly train again was frightening. But the thought that its crew was a gang of escaped criminals—coming back to haunt the Mountain Line—was simply too much.

Jack's footsteps echoed off the dark buildings so that he had the eerie sensation of being followed. A dog barked over by Elmer's Garage and Jack jumped. He looked around shyly to see if anyone was watching—as if anyone would be there at two in the morning.

Jack got to the east end of town where there were no street lights and none of the buildings were lit. Now he could see the vast spray of stars that had been blotted out by the lights of the town. He felt small and lonely under them.

By the time he reached the water tower he had taken off his jacket and tied it around his waist because he was too hot. Billie's car was parked beside the old platform. Its lights were out. Billie was dozing inside.

Jack rapped on the side window with his knuckles. Billie jumped, and banged her head on the steering wheel. Jack started laughing. It took a moment for Billie to catch her breath and unlock the door. Jack got in.

"Sorry about that," Jack said. "I didn't mean to scare you."

"On a night like this," she told him, "I have a hard enough time not scaring myself."

"So what's the plan?" he asked.

"We're going to send some mail," Billie said holding up a small backpack that had one of the shoulder straps missing. "I used to carry my books in this when I rode my bike to school. Let's put it up on the mail pole and see if the Eagle flies by."

The two of them got out of the car and scrambled up on the platform. It was about shoulder high and the wooden steps were missing, so they had to climb up the side. The platform smelled of sawdust and its planks creaked when they put their weight on them.

The shack that had once been on

top was gone. But a wooden pole with a metal arm that reached out toward the tracks was still mounted on the corner of the platform. They walked to it slowly, hoping that the old wood of the platform would not give way beneath them. The pole was a lot taller than Jack had expected; it was at least twelve feet high.

Billie looked up at the pole. "Now, how are we going to get this up there?"

Jack wrapped his arms around the pole and climbed up with his feet. The pole rocked a bit from side to side, but it seemed sturdy enough. He inched himself higher until he could pull himself up by the metal bar at the top.

"Be careful," said Billie, holding on to the cuff of his jeans, as though that would somehow help him. Jack pulled himself up the last few feet. He flung his leg over the metal arm and then sat on top of the pole looking down at Billie.

"Give me the backpack," he said, reaching down to her. She stood on her tiptoes holding it as high as she could.

"Just be careful, okay?" she told him.

Jack got a hold of the bag and steadied himself. He held the strap in his teeth and inched out on the metal bar until he could safely hang the bag on the end.

"What time is it?" he asked Billie.

Billie looked at her watch. "I can't read it. It's too dark."

Suddenly Jack felt a hot breeze like a breath on the back of his neck. He looked down along the tracks and saw that the stars in that part of the sky were blotted out by clouds of rising black smoke. The whistle sounded in the distance.

"Oh, God! Get down! Hurry!" Billie shouted beneath his dangling feet.

Jack grabbed the metal arm with both hands and swung down. His heart was pounding. He dropped to the tracks. His feet stung from the fall, and he fell to his knees. His back was to the approaching train. He could see his long shadow stretched along the tracks in the headlight of the Eagle.

Jack scrambled back on the shaking platform as the thunder of the train bore down on him. He and Billie tumbled to the back of the platform and lay face down as the blinding light and the screeching wheels shook them.

Jack looked up as the mighty engine passed the platform. He could see a man's arm catch the bag as the train passed, and suddenly the Eagle vanished. Billie raised her face.

The night was silent except for the creaking of the mail pole that was wobbling at the corner of the platform. The air was still and Jack could hear a dog barking down at the junk yard. Then, with a thud that made Billie scream, the bag landed in front of them—an old burlap mail sack tied closed with rope. On the side the words U.S. MAIL were written in black, and below that: THE EAGLE.

They lay there for a moment, and Jack could feel his heart pounding against the wooden planks beneath him. He caught his breath, and as the two of them were getting to their feet, he noticed that he was holding Billie's hand.

Chapter 7

"Wowee!" Bert said the next day when they brought the mail bag to the diner. He was excited like a little kid. He held the sack in front of him at arms' length, then pulled it in to hug it.

"This is a thing of beauty," he said. "So this was why you were interested in the train! Why, this is probably the only thing that remains of the Eagle. This should be in a museum or something. It must have been in your attic for more than a century."

"Well, it's yours," Billie said.

"Seriously?"

"Sure," Jack said. "No one else would appreciate it the way you would."

"Why, that's very kind of you," Bert said. "Very kind. I'll call the post office this afternoon to ask what I should do with all the letters." He folded the bag carefully, put it on a shelf, and then turned back to Jack and Billie. "Lunch is on me," he told them. "What'll it be? I'll make you anything you want."

While Jack looked at the menu, Billie asked Bert about the articles he had promised them.

"Oh, yeah," Bert said. "I got so excited I nearly forgot. I could only find one article in my scrapbooks."

Bert pulled a picture album from under the counter. He opened it to a page marked with a paper napkin. "It's right here," he said, turning the book on the counter so that the two of them could read it. "This article is one hundred years old tomorrow."

It was an old, yellowed newspaper page cut from the *Pine City Examiner*. Pasted above it was a postcard picture of the Eagle. The headline read, "Postal Locomotive Disappears." Jack and Billie leaned forward, and Billie began to read the article aloud.

"The Eagle, a steam locomotive for the United States Postal Authorities, vanished last night between the coastal town of Point Muir and the Central Valley Line.

"Postal authorities suspect its crew of derailing the locomotive and stealing its precious cargo: a shipment of jewelry valued at twenty-five thousand dollars.

"Based on the last sighting of the train outside the town of Black Diamond, law enforcement officials think that the locomotive was derailed into Morro Lake. They believe that its crew escaped on foot north to the Canadian border.

"Wanted in connection with the disappearance of the Eagle and its cargo are its crew: Alexander Winters. . ."

Billie stopped reading suddenly. She looked over at Jack with her eyes wide.

"Is that it? One person?" Jack asked.

"No, there are two more crew members. William Parker and Jack Ford."

Jack felt a chill go through him when he heard his own name.

"Let me see that," he said, grabbing the book. "That's my name."

"It's my name, too," Billie said. "William Parker—Billie Parker."

An hour later the two of them were sitting on the steps of Billie's front porch reading the columns of names in an old family Bible. At the heading of one of the columns was the word *Births*. Billie was running her finger down that column.

"One ... two ... three ... four. Four men named William in the last seven generations of my family," she said. Then she ran her finger down the column on the next page that was headed

Deaths. "And only three of them are listed here. One of them was born in 1862 and just disappears."

"So, you really think our great-great-grandfathers robbed a train and left their families?" Jack asked her.

"Well, it all adds up," Billy insisted. "We have the same names they had. We're the only ones that see the train. They're not haunting Black Diamond. They're haunting *us.*"

The thought gave Jack chills. "It was a hundred years ago tonight," he said. "With any luck the Eagle will vanish again."

"That would be a relief," Billie said. After a moment of silence she added, "But then we'd never know what's going on."

Jack looked up at the trees in the bright sunlight. There were little kids playing in the yard across the street. He couldn't believe that this was the same town that was so frightening at night.

Jack sighed and turned to Billie.

"We have to go out there," Jack said. "We have to be at the bridge tonight. I don't really want to go. I'm really scared. But deep inside I feel like we *have* to go."

Billie pulled her knees up under her chin and wrapped her arms around her legs. "I know," she said. "I know. I have the same feeling."

Chapter 8

Jack was waiting under the tree in Billie's front yard when she tiptoed out the door and quietly clicked it shut. They started walking along the middle of the street. Jack had his hands in his pockets. He felt Billie take his arm, and he looked over at her.

She smiled at him. "I'm kind of nervous," she said.

When they got to Maplethorpe Avenue, they started walking along the tracks away from Jack's house. It was a four-mile hike to Morro Bridge, but it was only twelve-thirty. They had plenty of time.

As they walked, Jack knew that the train would come from behind, and that made him nervous. Even though it wasn't due for a couple of hours, he kept glancing over his shoulder, hoping that he wouldn't see a light in the distance. The two of them didn't talk much. Jack wished he had brought his flashlight—with fresh batteries this time. It was much too dark with the pines towering above them on both sides. Who knew what might be watching them from just beyond the first trees?

Jack tried to whistle but his mouth was too dry. Billie held his arm tightly. She felt warm by his side. An owl called from among the trees on their right. Jack wished he was home in bed.

When they had walked about a mile, Billie started to say something and then stopped abruptly. Ahead of them Jack saw a figure disappear into the trees. The two of them froze.

"Was that a deer?" he whispered.

"No," Billie whispered back, tightening her grip on his arm. "I think it was a person."

"Nah, couldn't be a person," Jack said, hoping that he was right. "No one in their right mind would be out here at this time of night."

Billie laughed, nervously covering her mouth with her hand.

"Do you want to go back?" Jack asked her.

She was silent a moment.

"No," she said softly.

They began walking again.

Jack kept the corner of his eye on the patch of trees where the figure had disappeared. When they were even with it, he jerked his head around and saw a small boy dodge behind a tree. Jack picked up a rock and shouted into the shadows.

"Who is that?" Jack called.

There was no answer. Jack could see a head look out from behind a tree and disappear again.

"Look," Jack said, "I can see you there, so you'd better come out before I nail you with this rock."

Jack kept his eye on the tree and bent to pick up a bigger stone.

"Okay, okay," a voice came from behind the tree. "I was just out walking." The boy emerged from behind the tree. He was about ten years old.

"What are you doing out here in the middle of the night?" Billie demanded.

"I got lost," the boy said. "I just started riding my bike this afternoon, and somehow I got lost. My mom's going to kill me."

Billie waved for him to come closer, and the boy dragged himself out of the woods and stood in front of them.

"Where do you live?" Jack asked him.

"Willowbrook," the boy said.

"*Willowbrook?*" Billie said, amazed. "That's got to be fifteen miles south of here."

The boy shrugged.

"Where's your bike?" Jack asked.

The boy jerked his thumb behind him at the woods. "In there some-where."

Jack shook his head and laughed.

"What's your name?" Billie asked.

"Alex."

Billie looked at Jack and then back at the boy. "Not Alexander Winters?" she asked, naming one of the Eagle's crew.

The boy was silent a moment. He shifted his weight from one foot to another, his hands in his pockets.

"How did you know?"

Chapter 9

By one-thirty the three of them were nearing Morro Bridge. Jack could see its dark curve in the distance. Billie had told Alex everything they knew about the Eagle. The last mile or so the three of them had walked in silence. They were almost there now. Jack wasn't sure if what he was feeling was excitement or terror.

They couldn't see Morro Lake as they approached the bridge. Morro Bridge crossed high above the lake from one cliff to another. But as they came closer Jack could hear the sounds of water lapping against the rocks far below.

"Well, here we are," Jack said when

they reached the edge. "We might as well get comfortable." He sat down in a clearing off to the side of the bridge. Far below, the wind stirred the face of the black lake. Far above, the stars shone coldly.

"You guys got any food?" Alex asked.

"Well," Jack said when they were all huddled safely on solid ground, "whatever's going on, we're all here. The great-great-grandchildren of the Eagle's crew are present and accounted for."

As Jack spoke, they heard the first rumble of the train on the other side of the lake, and they saw the black smoke rising above the horizon. The light appeared creeping among the pine trees on the opposite cliff. Behind the light the massive black engine grumbled and snarled.

Jack noticed a shape on the bridge

moving towards them. It was about halfway across, and it seemed much too large to be a man. When the train curved up onto the bridge, the figure was caught in the engine's light.

It was a magnificent deer that raised his great antlered head to look behind him at the train. In the light, his great shoulders were outlined in brilliant white, and his huge antlers were like shaped ice. The deer stood motionless, half turned to meet the train.

The train saw him. It began to brake even before it mounted the bridge. The steel wheels froze and screeched on the rails. As the train skidded along, showers of sparks spilled from beneath the engine and disappeared into the darkness beneath the bridge. The shriek of steel echoed along the cliffs. Still the Eagle shuddered along the tracks.

The deer did not run. He stood tall and beautiful, his pointed ears twitching in the train's headlight.

The train was nearly upon the deer. Billie closed her eyes. The black train slowed and slowed and finally dragged to a stop a few yards from the handsome buck.

Jack saw the last two cars of the Eagle buckle and rise up from the rails because of the sudden stop. The train's caboose rocked back and forth and then tipped from the rail. The car's back end caught on the wooden planks a moment, and then it swung down off the bridge.

Jack watched in terror as the next car was pulled after the caboose. Both of them dangled there before the rest of the train toppled sideways.

The train plunged down—slowly down—toward the lake, twisting like a snake as it fell. Then a crash of water and mist rose high into the air. Jack stepped to the edge and watched the foaming water churn out in circles where the train had disappeared.

The great deer calmly walked to-ward them, its hooves clicking on the wooden bridge. It passed the small, stunned group of young people as though it did not see them. Then it bounded into the darkness of the forest.

Jack stood in silence. He understood now. The crew of the Eagle were not thieves. They did not leave their families and flee to Canada. They did not purposely destroy their own train. The three of them had innocently died in Lake Morro, trying to save the life of a deer.

The great-great-grandchildren of the Eagle's crew stood listening, across a century of silence, to the slapping of the water against the rocks below, and then the lake was still.

"They just wanted us to know," Billie said to Jack. "We're their great-great-grandchildren. We carry their names. They just wanted us to know that they were not bad men."

The three of them began the long walk back to Black Diamond.

Chapter 10

Back in Black Diamond the sheriff called the younger boy's family, and drove them all home just as dawn was breaking. Jack and Billie told their families their story. It was hard to know whether anyone believed them, but even Jack's brother Dean never teased him about it.

The next afternoon, Billie entered the death of William Parker in the family Bible—a hundred years late. Then Jack and Billie hiked, hand in hand, up to the bridge with some wild flowers. They tossed them into the lake below as a kind of late funeral. It made the two of them feel better.

Nights are quiet now in Black Diamond. Except for the occasional cry of a wolf or the screech of an owl, no sound comes from the forest where the Mountain Line lies. The tracks lie silent and cold among the trees in the moonlight.

Waiting.